Welcome to the neighbourhood! Let's meet the locals!

Introducing

Arthur
the Dachshund

Job Pet Detective "Sausage"

Fun Fact
Dachshunds are also known as sausage dogs, doxies, badger dogs and wieners.

Masha
the British Blue

Job Pet Detective "Mash"

Fun Fact

British Shorthair cats can also be bluecream, white, black, red, silver, cameo, and tortoiseshell.

Tumbler
the British Blue

Masha's brother

Gemma
the German Shepherd
Retired Therapy Dog

Pinkie
the Pug
Fashion Guru

Arthur's friends

The Squirrels

Darryl and Cheryl

Their kits:
Meryl, Laurel and Zeus

Viggo

the Hedgehog

ANIMAL CODE

LIVE BY THE CODE
FOR A BETTER COMMUNITY

No matter what size or breed,
Be a friend to those in need.

Whether the chore is big or small,
Lend a hoof, hand, foot, wing, claw
or paw to one and all.

Also by **Eva Bea Knight**

Sausage and Mash at Halloween
Sausage and Mash at Christmas
Sausage and Mash at Easter
Sausage and Mash on the Beach

Picture Book
Allegra the Worry Doll

Sausage and Mash Pawsome Pet Detectives

written and illustrated by
Eva Bea Knight

For Parker – whose honest opinions mean so much and always make me laugh!

Sausage and Mash Pawsome Pet Detectives
Text copyright © Eva Bea Knight 2024
Illustrations copyright © Eva Bea Knight 2024

Eva Bea Knight has asserted her right to be identified as the author and illustrator of this work under the Copyright, Designs and Patents Act, 1988.

All rights reserved. No part of this publication may be reproduced, stored in a retrieval system, or transmitted in any form or by any means, electronic, mechanical photocopying, recording or otherwise, without the prior permission in writing of the author.

This is a work of fiction.
Names, characters, businesses, places, events and incidents are either the products of the author's imagination or used in a fictitious manner. Any resemblance to actual persons, living or dead, or actual events is purely coincidental.

A catalogue record of this book is available from the British Library.

ISBN: 978-1-0686118-1-0

CONTENTS

1	When Arthur Met Masha	1
2	Becoming Pet Detectives	23
3	A Catchy Slogan	42
4	Operation Outfit	65
5	Operation Darryl	94
6	Operation Viggo	127
7	Operation Reclaim Outfit	143

Chapter 1
When Arthur Met Masha

Everyone in the Baker family was fast asleep except for Arthur, their sausage dog. For the humans, Mum, Dad, Della, Dylan and Daisy, it was another sleepy Sunday and no one was quite ready for what the day had in store. For Arthur, who was wide awake, it was the perfect time to listen to another audiobook.

This morning, he was listening to his favourite Sherlock Holmes adventure. Sherlock—

the world famous detective—had just caught the villain. Sherlock's friend, Dr Watson, who had been bumped on the head, woke up after Sherlock had solved the mystery.

'I should be a detective,' Arthur said to himself. He waddled into the living room and gazed at the tropical fish in the family aquarium. 'I'm a lot like Sherlock,' he told the fish. 'It's a shame that Dr Watson is as silly as a squirrel.'

Arthur wasn't a show-off: he really was an exceptional dog. At five years old, he was musical, sporty and well-read. The little hound spoke a good many languages. Of course, like all dachshunds, Arthur spoke English and German but he also spoke French and Spanish. In addition, he was fluent in all the local animal languages like

Bird, Cat, Fox, Hedgehog and Squirrel. He didn't particularly like speaking Squirrel because of all the rhyming slang he had to remember. In his spare time, he was learning more exotic languages like Penguin and Koala.

Dreamily, Arthur watched the fish in the aquarium make swirling patterns. Arthur couldn't speak Fish but his fishy friends were fantastic listeners. Arthur often told them stories about Sherlock Holmes, Hercule Poirot, Inspector Morse, Miss Marple, and other famous detectives from books and old TV shows.

Feeling hunger pangs, Arthur went to inspect his food bowl. How annoying! Staring at him was the same heap of dried-out vegetarian dog biscuits that his sister Della had given him yesterday! They were 100% meat free, 100%

tasteless, and smelled quite a bit like soggy seaweed.

To reduce her carbon footprint, Della had started a healthy eating campaign for the whole family. Arthur was fine with that. He would even award her Star of the Week. What really got up his snout was that Della believed she was a dog whisperer! SHE WASN'T! Arthur might be healthier but he wouldn't be happier without meat—he wanted to be a carnivore.

'If I was a detective,' Arthur told the fish, 'my first case would be Operation Disgusting Biscuits. I'd investigate why Mum and Dad let Della feed me these things. Are they cabbage? Are they spinach? Who knows, who cares?' he grumbled. 'All I know is that they shouldn't be fed to a pedigree dog like me.'

Although the fish had heard the same speech many times, Arthur didn't mind repeating it. Grumpily, the dog paced back to his second favourite spot: his downstairs bed, which was large and soft, and ideal for surveillance. It was here that Arthur spent many pleasant hours plotting how to catch the squirrels, who had the impudence to live in the oak tree at the end of *his* back garden.

'Life would be simpler if I were a fish,' Arthur sighed. He scampered over to the nearest mirror. Being a small bundle of attractiveness did get tiresome. Whenever he went walking in the park, children and grown-ups ahhed and oohed at his expressive brown eyes, flappy ears, long body, smooth amber coat, and miniscule (but sturdy) tan legs. 'What a sweet sausage dog!' they all exclaimed when Arthur wiggled past them. Humans were equally impressed by his on-trend clothes: his shiny raincoats, his onesies, his tartan jackets and his enviable collection of fabulous and quirky bow ties.

As a puppy, Arthur found the attention very gratifying. In those distant days, he didn't mind all the hands—the cold and clammy ones, the warm and chubby ones—that wanted to pat him. Then there were those people who asked if they could feed him a treat or tug his extra-large ears or poke his long snout. Mostly, he had liked all the fussing. Now, being treated like a pop star simply for being a tiny dog with awesome fashion sense was old news.

Being a mature dog, he wanted—he needed—more than human adoration and attention. Being cute was uncomplicated; it was as easy as chasing a cat up a tree. He wanted to do something important with the rest of his life.

Gentle rain tapped against the window, lulling Arthur into a mid-morning nap. Soon, he was wrestling a scurry of squirrels in a frenzied dream. After he'd scared them away, he imagined he was lapping up a gigantic bowl of succulent chicken in gravy. No matter how much he ate, the dish was always full. This was one of his favourite dreams and he replayed it over and over.

When it stopped raining, Arthur got up and went through his yoga routine. He lunged into three downward dog poses and two cobra poses to shake off his sleepiness. Now he was limbered up, he could attempt the giant staircase. Tongue hanging out, he bounced up the stairs. He hoped that his soulful eyes would inspire one of his humans to give him a decent breakfast.

He tiptoed into the first of the bedrooms where he heard Mum angrily telling Dad to roll over and stop snoring. Dad's snoring was horrible; it sounded like a beginner playing the trumpet, so Arthur escaped without delay.

Next stop was the bedroom belonging to his brother Dylan. He especially liked Dylan's room for its lingering odour of chicken nuggets, French fries, pizza and cheese tortillas. Once inside, Arthur crept under Dylan's bed, hoping to discover a leftover snack. Disappointed, his nose merely discovered a pair of muddy trainers and some smelly football socks.

Third stop on Arthur's checklist was his sister Daisy's room. When he poked his head inside, he saw something wonderful: SHE WAS AWAKE! But Daisy was in a world of her own, wearing her headset and clinging to her game controller. Like a crazy chimpanzee, she was jumping about trying to get to the next level of her digital adventure. Deafened by the noise and dazzled by the flashing lights, Arthur made another hasty retreat.

Last stop was Della's room. After a half-hearted push, Arthur realised that her door was blocked by a mountain of books and science magazines. Disheartened, Arthur listened to the symphony of snores, snuffles and electronic music that filled the upstairs hallway.

Operation Proper Breakfast had been a disaster! Arthur grimly realised that he would have to eat the stale biscuits in his bowl after all. Going downstairs, step by step, he began to feel optimistic. Last Sunday morning, he'd found some smoked ham from Dad's midnight snack under the fridge.

The bottom of the staircase was Arthur's greatest challenge; he had to launch himself off the biggest step like a daring Acapulco cliff diver. He'd done it! Some days he wobbled and splattered like jelly on the floor. Today, he landed with the skill of an Olympic gold gymnast. He was sorry that no one had seen it.

Suddenly, his sensitive hearing told him that he wasn't alone. Lifting one ear and then the other, Arthur heard a crunching sound coming from the kitchen. With a tilt of his head, he tuned in to the frequency: someone was eating his dog biscuits! Was it one of the squirrels? He had already warned those rodents to stay away from his dog door. Without delay, he raced into the kitchen.

'Stop right there!' Arthur thundered.

There at his food bowl lurked a dark figure.

'The game's up breakfast thief!' Arthur barked. 'Or rather brunch thief!'

The orange glow of autumn sunshine brightened the kitchen; gradually, the mysterious stranger came into view. It wasn't a squirrel...

IT WAS A CAT!

The cat's tail shot up like an exploded firework. Frozen like an ice sculpture, she stared at the miniature dog, who was glowering at her with the force of a ready-to-erupt volcano.

'What the blazes? Who are you and what are you doing here?' snarled Arthur, raising his brows.

Dog biscuit crumbs fell silently from the cat's whiskers onto the floor. If this had been an animal video, it would have been hilarious! But this was a real-life crime being committed in *Arthur's house* and he was fuming.

Secretly, the cat was plotting her escape. She calculated that one swipe of the dachshund's nose would distress him and buy her enough time to bolt out of the dog flap.

'Nothing to say for yourself, then?' Arthur sneered, feeling satisfied. He knew that cats were overrated and undertalented, empty vessels with fancy nails; no better than squirrels with pretty faces.

An eerie hush stretched across the room.

Feline eyeballs met canine eyeballs.

The fridge hummed.

The aquarium bubbled and whirred.

Time

    stood

        still...

'Well, let me tell you what I've deduced so far,' Arthur said crossly. 'You used *my* dog flap to enter the premises. You ate *my* brunch from *my* food bowl—notice it even has *my* name on it! In summary, you've committed two serious offences: breaking and entering and scoffing dog biscuits without permission.'

'Excellent deduction, *Sherlock*,' the cat admitted. Instantly, she noticed that this comment pleased the dog because his small chest inflated with pride. This bought her some thinking time. She knew about dachshunds: they were obstinate, mischievous dogs, fairly clever but mostly known for wearing fashionable clothes. This Arthur character probably had dozens of outfits in his collection. All she owned was a couple of plain and sensible collars that didn't interfere with her daily roaming around the neighbourhood. Yes, she knew all about these pedigree dogs who thought they were far cleverer than they were. Surely she could outsmart him?

'I want to apologise,' she began. 'You're quite right to be angry. I'd be angry too. But I'm guessing that you don't like these biscuits. The other day I found them lying on your lawn—so I ate them. I mean, why let the squirrels have them? Better me than them, don't you think?'

Clever cat-chat wasn't enough to excuse this criminal behaviour, Arthur decided. This cat was BUSTED! She was a sneaky food thief, although she did make some extremely good points (especially about the squirrels). Annoyingly, she spoke almost perfect Dog and she was right about the biscuits being on the lawn.

Arthur had a flashback to the biscuit incident. It happened last Monday when it was Della's turn to give him dinner. Still wearing her school uniform, Della was telling him to save the planet's resources and eat his biscuits. In a very reasonable way, Arthur was trying to explain to Della that the disgusting pellets were unsuitable for dogs and shouldn't even be fed to the fish. Unfortunately, because Della's understanding of Dog was only basic, she heard Arthur say this: 'WOOF, WOOOF, WOO-WOOF, GROWL, WHINE, WHIIIIINNE, WHISTLE.'

'Arthur, you're being fussy and ungrateful,' Della had snapped. 'I'm going to let the birds eat your dinner!' Then she had flung the biscuits straight out of the bowl and into the back garden.

The flashback was over. Arthur was back to the present and deep in his own thoughts. The cat noticed this and began to relax. She started to groom her fur, licking it smooth, giving Arthur a moment to observe her properly. He had already recognised her as a British Blue Shorthair. All the tell-tale characteristics were there: her eyes were amber, her body was muscular and her glossy coat was silvery grey-blue. Arthur's previous experience with this breed told him that they could be playful and resourceful. Perhaps she had some good ideas about banishing the squirrels from the back garden?

'I'm Masha Tawson,' the cat said, raising one of her paws. 'I live down the road.'

'Masha? That's a nickname for Maria, isn't it?' Arthur commented.

'That's right,' said Masha. 'And you're Arthur, like *King Arthur* and the Knights of the Round Table?'

'Not at all,' jeered Arthur. 'I'm named after Sir Arthur Conan Doyle who wrote the Sherlock Holmes books.'

The room grew quiet again; the gurgling of the aquarium crescendoed.

'Why do you like these horrible Della biscuits?' asked Arthur.

'I'm trying to be vegetarian,' explained Masha. 'Meat production has a huge impact on the environment.'

'I see,' said Arthur, remembering one of Della's environmental science projects.

'I want to do my bit,' Masha said. 'I'm not one hundred per cent vegetarian yet. It's been difficult. On Meaty Monday, my human mum fills my bowl with chicken, lamb, beef or duck. On Fishy Friday, my human dad gives me salmon, tuna, mackerel or trout...' She noticed that Arthur began to drool. 'By the way, do you speak Cat?'

Arthur's small chest inflated with pride again. 'Yes I do. Actually, I'm a polyglot, which means—'

'That you speak many languages,' interrupted Masha.

Arthur eyed her with suspicion. 'You're quite a well-educated cat. I've noticed that you speak fairly good Dog.'

'I have a thirst for knowledge and a spirit for adventure,' explained Masha, her whiskers dancing across her face.

Arthur's empty bowl glinted in the bright morning light.

'Hey, I have an idea,' said Masha excitedly. 'We can swap! Instead of Della's veggie biscuits I'll bring you my meaty and fishy dinners.'

Arthur grinned in anticipation: 'What a perfect solution!'

Human feet stirred upstairs and various voices darted across the bedrooms. It was time for Masha to leave so Arthur ushered his unexpected visitor to his dog door.

'You did a bad thing but for a logical reason,' he said. 'I'm prepared to forgive you. In fact, I'd go as far as saying you're nothing like the cats I generally cross paths with. They tend to be riff-raff.'

'We are all individuals,' Masha agreed. 'You're not exactly like other sausage dogs, are you?'

'Of course not! I'm absolutely unique,' Arthur said boldly.

Masha pushed her nose through the dog door. She felt warm sunshine on her whiskers. Just before she scampered away, she heard Arthur murmur, 'Don't forget tomorrow is Meaty Monday.'

Chapter 2
Becoming Pet Detectives

At Number 22, Arthur's household was organised chaos. There were hectic breakfasts, school runs and music lessons, sleepovers and noisy gaming, working from home, deliveries and endless phone calls to and from friends.

At Number 32, Masha had a quieter homelife. Her human mum was Pam Tawson, a retired secondary science teacher, and her human dad was Roy Tawson, who used to teach at a primary school. The Tawsons had a grown-up daughter who moved to Australia before Masha was born. Every Saturday, Pam and Roy made a video call to their three grandchildren in Australia. Masha liked listening to the grandchildren talk about school, swimming and surfing, Australian rules football and cricket.

The Tawsons were very kind to Masha. Her food was always freshly prepared, she could sleep anywhere in the house, and she could come and go as she pleased. Wherever Masha chose to sit, Roy would follow with a lint roller to clean up her fur. Like any good teachers, Pam and Roy treated every room like a classroom; everything went back to its proper place.

The Tawsons liked to learn about the world. When they learned a new language, Masha learned it too. When they watched an interesting documentary on TV or listened to a podcast, Masha would perch at one end of the sofa and learn all about history, geography and science. When the Tawsons played loud music, however, Masha made herself scarce. Pam and Roy especially liked singing karaoke. Sadly, they couldn't really sing in tune (not that Masha would ever tell them they howled like dogs with squashed paws).

Every Tuesday, Masha visited her brother, Tumbler, who lived at Number 50. Tumbler was a larger, greyer British Blue than his sister, with striking orange eyes. Tumbler lived with his two dads, Kwan, a busy dentist, and Phil, a pilot. Phil travelled so often that Kwan gave cooking classes in his free time. He had taught Pam and Roy how to make his grandma's special Korean recipes.

The day had arrived: it was Operation Meaty Monday. Once Pam and Roy had gone out to their art class, Masha wrapped her dinner in a napkin, clenched the "food delivery" between her teeth, and followed her usual route to Number 22. She clambered over walls and squeezed through broken fence panels to deliver Pam's traditional beef stew to Arthur. When a vixen became too inquisitive, she swiped the air with her lioness claws and warned her off.

On arrival, Masha waited patiently in the back garden. Soon, she heard Arthur's secret code (three short yaps). This told her that there were no Bakers in the house (except for Daisy, who

was upstairs and preoccupied with her game).

As Arthur greedily chomped through the delicious stew in the kitchen, Masha snooped around Arthur's living room. It was very different from her own: it was a glorious mess! Books, DVDs, CDs and magazines cluttered the shelves and were piled up on the floor. She noticed that the Bakers liked novels, thrillers, biographies, travel brochures, and detective magazines.

Boxes were stacked beside the radiators, sheet music lay under the coffee table, and papers littered the computer desk. In another corner, there was an upright piano, a recorder, a guitar, a half-drunk cup of tea, and a tablet with an empty bottle of lemon squash perched on top of it.

'This stew is so tasty!' Arthur called out from the kitchen. 'It's got just the right balance of tender beef and garden peas.'

Masha jumped onto the piano keys, and tiptoed across them to play a pop song she'd heard on the radio.

'I didn't know you played piano,' said Arthur, wolfing down the last of his stew.

'Tumbler and I are quite musical,' said Masha. 'I used to be in the cat choir. Tumbler still is, and he sings solos in the concerts. I stopped going to rehearsals because I got too busy exploring the neighbourhood.'

Arthur grimaced, recalling the memory of a recent cat concert. It had kept him awake and tortured his supersensitive ear drums. He had told

Tumbler's cat choir to 'shut up' then Mum had told him to 'be quiet' and go back to bed.

'Your living room is a shambles! It's every cat's dream!' squealed Masha.

Squeezing behind the velvet sofa, she discovered a pair of trainers, one flip-flop, a sparkly mitten, two squeaky toys and a meat-free dog chew. She had already calculated there were 39 potential hiding places for her to enjoy. She marvelled at the flowery fabrics, the mountain of cushions, and the striped Mexican floor rug. There were colourful oil paintings and family photos mounted higgledy-piggledy on the walls. In contrast, Masha's living room was all shiny and metallic; walls were magnolia and every picture was lined up perfectly.

The Bakers' aquarium was very impressive. Masha became mesmerised by the tropical fish gliding through the water, twinkling like fairy lights amongst the swishing carpet plants. She was aware of life going on upstairs too. She could hear Daisy stomping around and talking to a friend.

By the time Arthur came in, Masha was perched on the tallest tower of books. She was spying on the squirrels foraging for food in the back garden.

'This room is endless fun,' Masha sighed. 'It's such a fantastic mess! You could explore for hours in here!'

Instantly, Arthur took offence to Masha's comment. For a moment, he entertained the delicious thought of toppling her from the pile of books she was on and watching her crash to the ground. But he reminded himself that Masha was his guest, that she had just delivered a gorgeous beef stew, and that Fishy Friday was coming up.

'This room isn't a mess!' announced Arthur. 'It's an orchestra of odours, a potpourri of potential. I've catalogued every smell in here and stored it in my very extensive mental library. As a cat, you wouldn't understand, but it takes years for a dog to perfect their database. You smell something, you log it, you know it.'

Arthur was soon settled in his dog bed. He realised that a few meaty morsels were still stuck to the tip of his snout and the ends of his whiskers. Expertly, he reached them all with his tongue.

Masha jumped down from her book tower with the lightness of a butterfly. 'By my calculations, you live with five humans. Two adults and three children aged between seven and fourteen?'

'What evidence did you use to come to your conclusion?' Arthur probed.

'Family pictures, books, items of clothing, and what you've told me so far,' beamed Masha. 'Am I right?'

'No, you are not!' Arthur replied smugly. 'I live with two adults and three children aged between *eight* and fourteen *and a half*.'

A long silence enveloped the two animals. Suspicious eyeballs met suspicious eyeballs. For an awkward minute, both pets pretended to listen to the gurgle of the aquarium and the steady drip of the kitchen tap.

'You like mystery stories, don't you?' Masha said at last.

'Well, excuse me Dr Watson!' Arthur scoffed. 'You've cracked the case! Was it the books, detective magazines or audiobooks that gave it away? Even the squirrels could have solved that one!'

Masha felt her tail bristle: Arthur was so easily offended. Was he insecure about his miniature size? She disguised her annoyance by curling her tail under her bottom.

'Do you ever want more than this?' she asked him. 'Watching squirrels, waiting for walkies, sniffing out chicken and the odd football sock…?

'I have literature,' Arthur said sharply. 'I have Sherlock, Poirot, Miss Marple and all the other famous detectives.'

Masha's amber eyes flashed, her tail curled into a question mark, and her whiskers danced. 'What if *you* could be like Sherlock?' she asked slowly. '*Couldn't you be a detective* and do something useful and important?'

Arthur felt the rush of excitement. 'Solve mysteries?' he gasped. 'Do dangerous detecting?' He circled the room, his tail wagging. He went behind the sofa and reappeared with a banana chew toy, which he shook viciously and dropped on the floor. 'I've got it!' he exclaimed. 'I could start a detective agency! You could help me! You could be my Dr Watson!'

'But it was my idea,' Masha reminded him gently. 'We should be partners, shouldn't we? Two heads are better than one? Fifty-fifty?'

Arthur was no longer listening; he was imagining how dignified he would look in a detective outfit. Within days, he would probably set a new trend across the neighbourhood. Then every dog in every grooming salon across London would want a detective outfit too. Next, Arthur would become an international sensation, and dogs in Paris and New York would try to imitate him!

'I'll order my suit online,' he muttered.

'Paws of Gravile Row are sure to have a tweed cape and a deerstalker hat. It might even be eligible for express delivery, so I could have it by tomorrow. Oh yes, I'll soon be turning heads on Oxford Street *and* Bond Street!'

Masha could barely hide her irritation. She fantasised about slapping the little sausage dog with her tail. Why couldn't Arthur turn his attention away from fashion for just one minute? Were all dachshunds like this?

'We need cases,' she said seriously. 'If we want the detective agency to be a success, we need to tell other pets what we do. We need to make a business plan.'

Arthur hopped onto the office chair so that he could admire his reflection in a corner of the darkened computer screen. He wondered which tweed would bring out the chestnut flecks in his eyes.

Masha restrained her tail from thumping the ground impatiently. 'It's too soon for a website,' she continued. 'We'll start with word-of-mouth. My brother Tumbler knows everybody. Once we solve our first case then other pets will recommend us. But we need that something extra. What's our unique selling point? What makes us special?'

'Do you know of another pet detective agency around here?' asked Arthur sarcastically.

'No, I don't,' admitted Masha. 'So our unique selling point is that we're unique! There aren't any other pets out there doing what we do!'

'A good deduction,' Arthur agreed. He marvelled at how similar his profile was to that of Sherlock Holmes.

'It's not enough to just look the part,' said Masha. 'We'll need a name. It has to be catchy, easy to remember, amusing but not ridiculous. What should we be called?'

'A name… a name?' Arthur was back in his bed, sitting up with right paw raised ready for action. After a long pause, he suggested: 'Pets Against Crime.'

'That's a little bit wishy-washy,' she mused. 'It has to be awesome… It has to be paw-some!'

'Very clever,' remarked Arthur. 'A play on words. "Pawsome" rather than "awesome" ... We could call ourselves "Bark and Purr" or "Sniff and Scratch" or –'

'I've got it!' exclaimed Masha with flashing eyes. 'Let's be *Sausage and Mash*!'

Chapter 3
A Catchy Slogan

Arthur didn't approve of 'Sausage and Mash' as the name of a detective agency. He almost missed out on Fishy Friday because he went into a sulk. But the thought of Roy's poached, bone-free mackerel changed his mind, and he agreed to meet Masha outside his garden shed.

Sunset was creeping in, setting the lawn ablaze with twinkly orange light, painting the windows of the house fiery red.

Waiting for Masha to arrive, Arthur lifted his nose to sample the air: it was a perfume of damp soil, fragrant rose petals and the unmistakable odour of scandalous squirrels.

Masha arrived with a carefully wrapped food parcel and laid it down by Arthur's sturdy legs. Never mind starting a detective agency, she thought to herself, perhaps she should start an online food delivery service called Sausage Dogs Eat Free.

'Your vegetarian biscuits are over there,' Arthur said to Masha, tilting his head at a nearby food dish.

Both pets ate in silence.

'It's such an awful name,' Arthur said at last. 'You said "amusing not ridiculous" and now we're named after a breakfast or brunch item. Sausage and Mash is pub grub or "Today's Special" at the local cafe. I'm partial to a juicy pork sausage and some buttery mash but it's not the name of a serious detective and his assistant.'

'I disagree with you,' said Masha. 'It's a good name that's as British as Sherlock Holmes, a cup of tea, the Tower of London...'

'We might just as well call ourselves "Fish and Chips" or "Tea and Biscuits" then!' Arthur bellowed.

'Calling ourselves "Sausage and Mash" tells pets that we're traditional and reliable,' reasoned Masha. 'All we need now is a slogan.'

'Why do we need a slogan?' Arthur growled.

'Every business—especially a new one—needs a slogan,' insisted Masha.

'Don't tell me, it has to be catchy and easy to remember?' Arthur snapped.

Masha narrowed her eyes at him.

'If you insist on a slogan, then I have the perfect one,' said Arthur theatrically. He cleared his throat then offered: 'We have the skills to cure your ills.'

'I'm not sure about that one,' Masha frowned. 'It makes me think of a doctor's surgery. Besides, we have to sound clever *and* modern.'

'I'm sorry I'm so old-fashioned,' Arthur said glumly.

'Have you ordered your deerstalker hat and tweed cape yet?' Masha said, changing the subject.

'No, as it turns out,' sighed Arthur. 'I couldn't get on the internet. I'll have to make do with my shiny new raincoat and a bow tie for now.'

'Well, that'll look smart and professional,' said Masha.

'Flattery will get you nowhere,' Arthur lied. 'You're a sly one,' he added. 'I should've known I'd have trouble going into business with a cat.'

'Sausage and Mash are in business then?' said Masha, bursting with pride.

'Yes, we're in business,' agreed Arthur. 'So apart from a slogan, we'll need an office.'

'Meeting at mine might be difficult,' said Masha without batting a whisker. 'Two retired teachers, who like gardening and DIY. They'll only get in our way.'

'It couldn't be at your house anyway,' said Arthur. 'Unlike you, I can't just go roaming around the neighbourhood until dark. People notice if I go missing. What we need is a quiet space, out of the way, but convenient to both of us. I must consider this in greater depth.'

Masha watched Arthur waddle down the path all the way to the oak tree. Feeling a splash on her whiskers, she took cover beside the Bakers' garden shed. She'd been up on the roof for a nap and a sunbathe but she hadn't noticed very much about the building before. On closer inspection, she realised that it was less like a shed and more like an elaborate office.

Peeking through the double glass doors, she could see a sofa, an armchair, a small table, and a shelf lined with books and board games. In another corner, there was what Pam and Roy liked to call "a tea station" with a kettle, a mini fridge, and glass jars filled with assorted biscuits, instant coffee and teabags.

'Who uses this place?' asked Masha.

'Everyone,' said Arthur. 'Especially in the summer. Mum does yoga in there. Dad and Daisy play board games in there. Then there's the odd music lesson. If Dylan needs a time-out after an argument, he goes in there. Della takes her laptop in there when she's revising. But it can get draughty and humans don't like spiders...'

Masha checked her claws and waited patiently for Arthur to come to the same conclusion she'd come to five minutes earlier. Still as a sphinx, she waited. Finally, she gestured towards the construction beside her and Arthur did a double take.

'I've got it!' he exclaimed. 'This marvellous place can be my office—I mean, *our* office. It's even got a dog—*and cat*—flap.'

'Of course! What a brilliant idea!' agreed Masha, trying to sound surprised.

'There's lots of natural light and it's very comfortable,' said Arthur, peering through the window and spotting one of his favourite cushions. He pushed his nose through the dog flap and knew that inside lurked a half-eaten bag of roast beef flavour crisps and a cup of cold chicken soup. 'So that's sorted,' he said, and wondered if it was too soon for his next nap.

'Are we going to charge clients for our services?' wondered Masha.

'I'm not sure,' puzzled Arthur. 'I'm more interested in the thrill of solving mysteries and gaining a reputation.'

'And looking good in the news?' chuckled Masha.

'One must maintain a professional appearance,' Arthur retorted.

'We could get paid with treats!' Masha said. 'Healthy, vegetarian ones.'

'Well, we can decide on the finer details later,' Arthur muttered. 'But I'd be open to receiving treats as a form of payment.'

Abruptly, both pets became aware that they were being watched. A pair of eyes glistened from the depths of the lavender bush. Arthur's snout told him all he needed to know: a middle-aged squirrel was hiding in there.

'Come out, squirrel, and show us what you're made of!' demanded Arthur.

A guilty-looking squirrel leapt out from the shrub. 'Alright, you got me!' he conceded.

'Don't worry,' Arthur told Masha, 'I'll translate what he says.'

'Thanks but I speak some Squirrel,' Masha assured her pet detective partner. 'I learned it as a kitten.' She looked at the glassy-eyed rodent and added: 'And you don't have to worry because I don't hunt squirrels.'

'Yeah, yeah, I already know that,' said the squirrel, offering her a twitchy smile.

'How do you know?' asked Masha.

The squirrel's bushy tail swished left and right like a windscreen wiper. 'I know lots of fings. Like, I know your name is Masha and you're Ahfur and I reckon it's because you're 'alf a dog. Get it? HALF A DOG!'

The squirrel waited for the laugh that never came.

Arthur grew impatient. 'I'm a dachshund, a noble breed, and I don't like your tone. Now stop wasting my—I mean, *our*—time.'

Like most dachshunds, Arthur distrusted squirrels. They were wild, scruffy, and made clicking sounds. This one had acorn shells in his tail and bird seed on his whiskers.

'Did you want to tell us something important?' asked Masha.

The squirrel mustered up his courage and nodded slowly.

'Well?' snapped Arthur.

'All the fings I've been hiding for winter are MISSING!' the squirrel moaned. 'I put my stash next to the compost 'eap at Number 40. It was the best collection on the street!'

'What items are missing?' Arthur asked him, growing curious.

'Oh, I 'ad some gorgeous daffodil bulbs, juicy fungi, and crunchy nuts. It was a proper, special stash! Really deluxe.'

Arthur raised his eyebrows. 'Another squirrel wanted it for himself,' he remarked, 'and stole it once he was sure you'd gone home.'

'Nope,' said the squirrel. 'All the squirrels round 'ere are mates of mine.'

'And why do we need to know about your stash?' enquired Arthur.

'I'd like Mash 'n' Sauce to investigate for me,' explained the squirrel.

Masha tried to hide a giggle. 'We're actually *Sausage and Mash*.'

Arthur was losing what was left of his patience. 'I don't think this is Sausage and Mash business,' he said. 'Squirrels squabbling over mouldy food isn't what I'd consider a case for professional detectives.'

'Oh please, my three kits are counting on me,' the squirrel pleaded. 'You wouldn't want their little tummies to go empty, would ya?'

'No, we wouldn't want that,' Masha said sympathetically. 'Tell us something about yourself.'

'I'm Darryl,' smiled the squirrel. 'Back at the nest, there's Cheryl, the light of me life, and Meryl and Laurel, our two ribbons and curls.'

'These rhyming patterns are so tiresome,' sighed Arthur. He turned to face the squirrel. 'So you have a *wife* named Cheryl and two *little girls* named Meryl and Laurel. Didn't you say you had *three* kits?'

Darryl twitched nervously. 'Oh, of course,' he added, 'there's Zeus, me pride and joy!'

'Your *little boy's* named *Zeus*!' gasped Arthur. '*Zeus*, the most powerful god of the Ancient Greeks, who zapped people with lightning bolts... Surely that's a dog's name!'

Masha tutted. 'Arthur, you're being a bit tactless,' she whispered. 'I could always take this case on my own. Lots of good detectives work solo.'

Embarrassed, Arthur fell silent.

'Pawsome Pets Smashin' Crime!' exclaimed Darryl.

The pet detectives turned to face the cheerful squirrel.

'I fink "Pawsome Pets Smashin' Crime" should be your slogan,' said Darryl. 'I know it's a good 'un.'

Masha beckoned for Arthur to follow her into their new office. They returned a moment later.

'My detective partner likes your slogan,' Arthur announced. 'Of course we plan to add "g" to "smashin" and then we'll use it.'

'So you'll 'elp me?" Darryl asked hopefully.

'Leave your winter food problems with us,' Masha said with a purr. 'This is a good neighbourhood and we want it to stay that way.'

'You are a couple of upright geezers,' said Darryl gratefully. 'And you really look the business!'

'Geezers? Look the business?' mused Arthur, forgetting his Squirrel.

'Yeah, look the business, dressed to impress and all that,' explained Darryl. 'I mean, Masha's got that posh fur coat and you're looking so sharp! That bow tie's a right stunner!'

Arthur puffed out his chest. He was about to explain that today's bow tie was one of the most charming in his entire collection when three junior squirrels, who looked identical to Darryl, jumped out from the lavender bush. Without delay, Darryl stood tall as a sergeant major. He gave three clicking commands so that his offspring formed an orderly queue. In a series of hops and skips, the junior squirrels followed their dad down the garden path.

Once all the squirrels were completely out of sight, Masha squealed: 'We just got our VERY FIRST CASE!' She raised her paw at Arthur to celebrate with a high five but all four of his sturdy feet remained stubbornly planted on the ground.

'I'm not sure this is what I had in mind,' grumbled Arthur. He tried to ignore Masha's dancing whiskers and bright mood. 'Squirrels are rascals! They'd steal biscuits from a baby's picnic.'

'Let's give Darryl a chance,' suggested Masha. 'We should try and treat all animals fairly, even those who live in the wild and aren't lucky enough to have our creature comforts.'

'Della would call that diversity,' remembered Arthur.

'Plus, we are going to have so much fun!' Masha said. 'There'll be a daring garden stakeout and then wham-bam-boom, we'll catch the food stash thief!'

For now, Arthur was consoled. 'We'll take the case,' he agreed. 'But that doesn't make me a fan of squirrels.'

After a few drops of rain plopped down on her whiskers, Masha said goodbye and skipped away, disappearing through a gap in the fence.

'Pawsome Pets Smashing Crime,' Arthur grumbled aloud. 'I still think that, given a little longer, I would have come up with something better.'

Feeling pleased with himself, he toddled back indoors. Tonight, he planned to take out seven of his favourite bow ties and decide which one best suited going on a daring night mission.

Chapter 4
Operation Outfit

Arthur was patiently waiting for Dylan to finish his tricky online maths homework.

'Are you any good at geometry?' Dylan asked his pet, pointing at the laptop.

Of course, Arthur knew how to find the area of an isosceles triangle but Dylan didn't speak advanced Dog so Arthur kept quiet.

At last, Dylan invited Arthur onto his bed so that they could search their favourite websites for pet clothes and accessories. They looked at waterproof coats, reflective jackets, colourful bandanas, designer t-shirts and dazzling collars. But Arthur didn't want any of these: he wanted a tweed cape and a deerstalker hat so that he could look like his hero Sherlock Holmes.

'How about a novelty pirate costume?' suggested Dylan.

Luckily, before Arthur could complain, Dad called Dylan downstairs to unload the dishwasher. Finally, Arthur was alone with Dylan's laptop. Skilfully, he pawed through the webpages until he found the perfect outfit. SUCCESS! Paws of Gravile Row had the ABSOLUTELY PERFECT tweedy fleece jacket and miniature deerstalker hat in their Autumn sale! AND it was eligible for express delivery, which meant it would be with him the following day. Tail wagging gleefully, Arthur's paw hovered over the Buy Now button. But before he could complete the purchase, Dylan burst back into the room, scowling and muttering about something being unfair. He dived onto his bed, snatched back his laptop and asked Arthur (rather impolitely) to leave him alone.

Back downstairs, Arthur decided Operation Outfit was far from over. He complained to the tropical fish that he never got enough access to the internet. In a quiet corner, Arthur leafed through a detective magazine to find a picture of Sherlock Holmes wearing his famous outfit. Minutes later, he was interrupted by the deafening sounds of a metronome and the pounding of piano keys. Daisy was practising her scales in between noisy slurps of her raspberry-banana smoothie.

'Here's the outfit I want,' Arthur said to Daisy, dragging his magazine under her feet and tapping it with his nose. 'Can you help me buy it online?'

All that Daisy heard was: 'WOOF! WOOF! HOWL! WHISTLE!'

She slammed the piano lid shut, and almost knocked Arthur over in her sprint back upstairs.

'Not now,' said Della, when Arthur ambushed her at the front door. She didn't even notice the magazine clenched between his teeth because she was weighed down with her heavy school backpack and a muddy hockey stick.

Mum was sitting at the breakfast bar, sorting out a guest list for her upcoming Big Birthday party. She didn't look down at him or his magazine but she promised, 'Daddy will take you for a walk.' She patted Arthur lovingly on the head and said, 'John, darling, take our little Arthurkins for a walk please. I've got so many emails to send.'

The last thing Arthur wanted in the middle of Operation Outfit was a walk but if it pleased Dad then he would go. All along the high street, Dad listened to rock music on his earphones. He played air guitar and hummed the chorus (Arthur was very embarrassed). Some of the shoppers and a passing cyclist mentioned that Arthur was "adorable". The dapper dachshund had no time for compliments; he was thinking about his detective outfit.

Once they got to the park, Dad let Arthur off his lead, turned up the volume on his phone, and began springing into star jumps. Arthur dashed off, looking for familiar faces. He found his friend, Pinkie, the fashionable pug, near one of the exits. Whenever he and Pinkie got together, they liked to talk about new clothes and grooming salons. Today, Pinkie was wearing his new rainbow sweater. He gave Arthur a few compliments about his denim coat and stripey bow tie.

'I think it's absolutely fabulous that you're going to be a detective!' gushed Pinkie. 'And I can't wait to see that new tweed cape!'

Eventually, the two little dogs were joined by their friend Gemma, an elegant German Shepherd. Arthur liked Gemma very much but she tended to talk mostly about St Joseph's Primary School, where she used to be a therapy dog. When she wasn't gushing about the 'fantastic children at St Joseph's', she was complaining about the painful arthritis in her left hip.

Pinkie had to leave the park early because he was going away for the weekend.

This left Arthur and Gemma alone. As expected, Gemma wanted to tell Arthur all about the smart new uniforms at St Joseph's. After a few minutes, Arthur decided he would also need to make his excuses.

'Gemma, it's been a pleasure chatting,' he said, 'but Dad will be wondering where I've got to.'

Actually, Arthur didn't go straight back to Dad. He wanted to follow a wasp into some long grass. Moments later, he heard two unfamiliar dogs playing a frantic chasing game. One of the dogs had the unmistakable accent of a Pembroke Welsh Corgi. Eventually, the game of tag grew louder as the two dogs got closer.

Arthur turned around slowly. He found himself nose to nose with a small, reddish-brown dog with the same oversized ears nature had blessed him with. He could have been looking at his own reflection in the bathroom mirror. HE WAS STARING AT ANOTHER DACHSHUND!

'Well, well, this is lush!' said the corgi, switching back and forth between the two sausage dogs like a judge at a talent contest. 'You two could be twins!'

On closer examination, Arthur noticed that this other sausage dog wasn't quite up to his own pedigree proportions. The other dachshund was quite a bit smaller, he had a longer snout, a slight bulge on his forehead, and extra wrinkles under his chin. But to any human—or corgi—he and the stranger were cookie-cutter clones of one another.

'I don't believe we've met,' said Arthur. 'Are you two just visiting the area?'

'No, we're local,' explained the corgi. 'We moved into the neighbourhood over the summer. I'm Lewis and my pal here is Jim.'

'I like your denim coat,' said Jim, staring at Arthur. 'I'd look like a cool surfer in that. Where'd you get it? I want one just like that. Lewis, don't you reckon I should get a coat like that? I've got an orange jacket, a red coat, a yellow t-shirt, a onesie and stripey pyjamas. But no denim coat.'

'My sausage friend has so much energy,' giggled Lewis. 'He's such a bundle of fun! He's lush! We've grown up together. We're like brothers, he knows the best games! He can even do funny stunts! Wanna see one?'

'I can't stay to chat,' said Arthur firmly. 'I'm ordering something online so that it'll arrive by tomorrow. Sorry but I'll have to run.'

'What is it?' asked Jim breathlessly. 'I bet it's cool. Is it a collar? A tin of biscuits? Is it cheese? I bet it's a whole packet of cheese. What kind of cheese is it? Is it cheddar? That's my favourite! Or is it Gloucester cheese? That's my second favourite. Or is it a zebra costume?'

'It's not any kind of cheese nor is it a novelty costume! It's my Sherlock Holmes outfit,' asserted Arthur. 'A tweedy cape and a deerstalker hat. I'll be wearing it when I do my detective work.'

'Ooh, why can't I get a Shylock Phones outfit?' whined Jim. 'Lewis, I'd make a lush detective, wouldn't I?'

'You'd be so lush,' Lewis agreed with a yelp. Then he whispered: 'A lot lusher than this boyo.' He and Jim began to wrestle one another in a new game of tag.

If he'd had time, Arthur would have advised his fellow dachshund to listen more and speak less. But he didn't have time. 'I have to go,' he said, and ran away as quickly as his short but sturdy legs could carry him.

Arthur found Dad doing his warm-down on the tennis court. On their walk home, Arthur had a spring in his step. He was eager to get back, eat his dinner, and resume Operation Outfit.

Later the same night, Arthur took up his position outside Dylan's bedroom. His extraordinary hearing told him everything he needed to know: Mum and Dad were in the kitchen making a shopping list for the Big Birthday party; Della was finishing her recycling poster in the study; and Daisy was in the living room watching a movie about robots.

On cue, Dylan came out of his bedroom and went into the bathroom for a shower.

As stealthily as a ninja snake, Arthur glided into Dylan's bedroom and found the open laptop on the floor. Luckily, Dylan hadn't remembered to close the Paws of Gravile Row tab from earlier. In the twitch of a whisker, Arthur had clicked on the Buy Now button and selected the Express Delivery option. IT WAS DONE! The detective outfit was his and would be arriving the very next day.

Tiptoeing out of Dylan's bedroom, Arthur floated down the stairs and slid off the bottom step like melted ice cream. Life was good. There was still enough time for an audiobook before bed.

The next day, Masha met Arthur inside the new Sausage and Mash headquarters. She had spent the morning investigating the back garden of Number 40 and wanted to share some intel about Darryl's missing stash of winter food.

'This garden office is perfect for us,' Masha beamed. 'It's so comfortable. I don't know why the Bakers let a few spiders scare them away.' She sat regally in a sphinx pose, warmed by a shaft of sunlight streaming through the glass doors.

Arthur was restless; he paced the floor. Preoccupied with his home delivery, he kept one ear raised like an antenna in the direction of the house.

'With your hearing, you definitely won't miss the doorbell,' Masha assured him. 'So first thing on our agenda is Darryl, don't you agree?'

'Yes, yes, the first item on the Sausage and Mash agenda is Darryl Squirrel's stolen items,' Arthur answered distractedly. Drifting into a daydream, he wondered if his deerstalker hat would be the exact shade he'd seen on the Paws of Gravile Row website.

'I checked on Darryl's hiding hole,' Masha was saying, 'and the food has definitely been stolen again. Darryl, his wife Cheryl, and the whole family are very upset.'

'A badger or a fox maybe?' Arthur said, imagining that he had heard the chime of the front doorbell.

'Badgers are rare in these parts. A hedgehog is more likely,' said Masha. 'I came across a hedgehog's nest a few gardens along from Number 40.' She felt the prickle of excitement in her tail. 'We'll plan a daring stakeout! I can hardly wait!'

'I know, it's thrilling!' cried Arthur. 'I can sneak out during Mum's Big Birthday party—I won't be missed at all. The food thief, whoever it is, had better watch out!'

Masha suddenly remembered something else. 'It's a funny thing,' she began, 'but on my way over, I saw a corgi with a dachshund. For a minute, I thought it was you with a new friend. I even shouted out your name. When the sausage dog ignored me, I realised that it wasn't you after all.'

'Of course it wasn't me!' barked Arthur. 'It's a dog called Jim. Next time, please be more observant. That nasty hound has a very long snout, a bumpy head, a saggy chin and terrible taste in fashion. He's so last season!'

'How do you know this Jim?' asked Masha.

'I had the misfortune of meeting him and his friend Lewis in the park,' spluttered Arthur. But he didn't want to stop there, he wanted to share all his thoughts about the new dog in town. 'Jim is possibly one of the most irritating canines I've ever met! He talks faster than a greyhound runs. His grammar is sloppy! No one seems to have told him that it's really rude to stare. He has such appalling manners, especially for a dachshund.'

'I'm sorry, Arthur,' said Masha quietly. 'It sounds like Jim needs to work on his behaviour before he gives dachshunds a bad name. And I know what you mean, you don't want anyone to let the team down. I wouldn't like to meet a British Blue who couldn't climb or follow maps.'

All of a sudden, Arthur heard a delivery van pull up outside the front of the house followed by footsteps and the familiar ding-dong of the doorbell.

'It's here! My outfit is here!' Arthur exclaimed. 'Wait for me, Masha! I want you to be the first to see it!'

He raced back towards the house. He miscalculated, though, and bashed his nose on the dog door. Ignoring the painful sting on his snout, he rushed through the kitchen, looking for someone to open the front door. Eventually, he found Mum in the living room, talking to Granny on the phone. When he barked, Mum shushed him, and gestured that she was busy but would open the door in a second. More of Arthur's barking brought Della out of her bedroom, holding a textbook and looking exasperated.

'Dylan, it's your turn to open the door!' she said. 'I'm trying to revise!' She disappeared into her room again.

A few whistles and whines later, Dylan emerged from his bedroom. Standing at the top of the stairs, looking sleepy, he asked: 'Yeah? What is it? Is there someone at the door?'

Arthur had planted himself at the foot of the stairs. From there he could see the unmistakable silhouette of the home delivery man through the frosted glass. The man rang the doorbell again and stooped down to leave the box—Arthur's precious box—on the doorstep.

Mum said goodbye to Granny, slipped her mobile phone into her pocket, and called out for Arthur. When she found him, she tickled the top of his head and apologised for leaving him waiting. The small dog panted and wagged his tail at the prospect of Mum FINALLY opening the front door. But Mum still wasn't ready; she stooped down to pick up a leaflet lying carelessly on the mat.

Time stood still… Arthur watched Mum read all about how to donate unwanted clothes to a local charity.

Arthur's impatience reached boiling point. Didn't Mum know that he was in the middle of a business meeting with Masha? Didn't she realise that he planned to change into his new detective outfit before going back to headquarters?

'You're a good boy, Arty-Smarty,' cooed Mum. 'You're the best guard dog, even though you're teeny. Now, let's see what all the commotion is about.'

At last, Mum put the leaflet away. Arthur whistled wildly and barked expectantly. He felt ready to burst with excitement as though he was about to have an extra birthday party. At the exact moment Mum's hand moved towards the door knob her mobile phone buzzed. She took the mobile out of her pocket and read a new text. She chuckled, unaware that she was wasting yet more time. Arthur wanted to get changed and make his grand entrance into the Sausage and Mash office. Masha wasn't fashionable but she did have style. Surely, even she would notice the quality of the fabric?

MUM OPENED THE FRONT DOOR.

'How strange,' she said. 'There's nothing here. Maybe it was a delivery for the neighbours? Oh well, I don't think we were expecting anything.'

WHAT? THE PARCEL WAS GONE? Arthur's jaw hung open in disbelief. He knew Mum was WRONG! There had been a delivery for *him…* but it had vanished! Before Mum could even think about closing the front door, Arthur had leapt into the front garden and charged down the path.

The wooden gate had been left open. Arthur knew the delivery man well and he always closed it behind him. The gate squeaked and slammed on the post as the wind blew it back and forth.

Frantically, Arthur scanned the street. The delivery van had long gone and there wasn't a soul in sight. His supersensitive snout picked up no clues. Mum insisted that he come back inside so he reluctantly plodded towards the front door.

Confused and sad, Arthur meandered back to the Sausage and Mash office, trying to make sense of what had just happened.

'Stolen!' Masha exclaimed. 'I don't believe it! This is such a good neighbourhood.

You really think it was taken from right under your nose? But why? Who would want to steal a tiny dog outfit?'

Slowly, the name began to form in Arthur's mind: J-I-M. JIM!

Chapter 5
Operation Darryl

Fishy Friday brought the pet detectives back together again. Despite the cold, damp weather, Arthur's afternoon was brightened by the delicious salmon brought to him by his dependable detective partner, Masha.

'Please convey my compliments to Roy,' said Arthur. 'This salmon is cooked to perfection. It's melt-in-the-mouth delicious and the sauce could win a prize!' He lapped up every tasty morsel.

The detective duo then turned their attention to other important business.

Looking for the ideal spot inside headquarters, Arthur got comfortable on the fluffy towel that his mum had thrown over a yoga mat, and Masha jumped onto the cosy armchair.

'Let's begin with Operation Stolen Package,' Masha proposed. 'I know it's a very sore subject for you, Arthur. Why do you think Jim's the culprit?'

'He's ill-mannered and impatient,' said Arthur.

'Plenty of pets are ill-mannered and impatient but they don't turn to a life of crime,' Masha cautioned him.

'It was his attitude,' replied Arthur. 'Jim hounded me—if you'll pardon the pun—*hounded* me about my personal life. He pestered me about my purchases and wanted everything I had.' He paused for breath. 'Although, curiously, I never told him my name or even hinted about where I lived.'

'Finding out where you live isn't difficult,' Masha reasoned. 'We're getting fairly well-known as Sausage and Mash. And I did see them in the neighbourhood that day. The evidence suggests that Jim and Lewis are the likeliest suspects.'

'The worst thing is, if Jim does have my detective outfit, it's all wrong for him,' groaned Arthur. 'The deerstalker hat won't sit right on that strange, bulging head of his.'

'He clearly wants to imitate your style,' suggested Masha.

'I am known as a trendsetter,' agreed Arthur.

'Leave Operation Stolen Package with me for now,' Masha decided. 'I'll put Lewis and Jim under my cat radar.'

'I'd appreciate that,' Arthur said.

'Don't mention it. A crime's been committed and we're the pawsome pet detectives who *smash* crime.'

'I wish I'd thought of that slogan rather than Darryl Squirrel,' muttered Arthur.

'Darryl isn't that bad,' said Masha. 'There are probably as many differences between squirrels as there are between sausage dogs. Just look at you and Jim, both dachshunds but with a hundred differences.'

'Closer to a thousand!' bellowed Arthur.

'Your mum's Big Birthday party is tomorrow,' Masha reminded him. 'Darryl and one of his kits are meeting us in the back garden at Number 40. So I'll pick you up around 10:00 p.m.'

Arthur became anxious. 'Oh, cheddar cheese crumbs! That's *so* late! Don't forget, my eyes aren't half as good as yours. Especially after dark. Plus, I'm not as young as I used to be, you know.'

'You're not that old,' Masha said encouragingly. 'Anyway, I'll be your guide. It's only nine gardens away. All of them are pretty bright, apart from Number 38.'

'I wish I already had my detective outfit,' Arthur admitted. 'I wanted to look like a real investigator for my first mission.'

'Clothes don't make the detective. You'll be fine,' said Masha, like a big sister.

It was almost time for the Big Birthday party to begin. Like actors changing their costumes backstage, the Bakers were rushing around getting ready for their guests. Mum was applying her lipstick; Dad was shaving; Dylan was gelling his hair; and Daisy was playing on her tablet. Only Della found time to take Arthur out for a short walk and, for that, the little dog was grateful.

Della put on her long, muddy raincoat to cover her party outfit and practised her Spanish verbs on the way to the park. She picked Arthur up a few times to hurry him along; he enjoyed the unexpected puppy treatment.

'Just a quick run, Arty-Smarty,' Della told him when they got to the park. As soon as he was unleashed, Arthur bolted. He galloped past the children's playground and the basketball court, and dove into the long grass. He was eager to catch another glimpse of Lewis and Jim. Disappointingly, neither scoundrel was anywhere to be seen. No doubt, they were helping themselves to another parcel somewhere else in the neighbourhood.

That evening, the party started on time. Arthur knew that he'd have to duck and dive to avoid being stepped on. Different faces stooped down to say hello to him. He was patted by an auntie, prodded by a little cousin, and complimented by an uncle. Granny cuddled him on the sofa, and fed him a whole sausage roll. When she got up for more wine, Arthur hopped off the sofa, and crept under the dining table.

He had to work fast because it was already 9:58 p.m. and he knew that Masha was never late. Glasses clinked, forks scraped plates, people chattered and tittered, and

Daisy's tablet whistled. This was a no-brainer: Arthur had the perfect opportunity to escape.

Unfortunately, at 9:59 p.m., Dad asked everyone for their attention, and the room grew silent. Whenever it was Mum's birthday, Dad liked to give a speech about how he and 'beautiful, intelligent Sarah' had first met.

Arthur was scuppered; he sank lower under the table, cringing at Dad's cheesy jokes. The end of the story was greeted with cheers and a round of applause.

NOW WAS ARTHUR'S MOMENT!

The stealthy dachshund tiptoed from the living room to the kitchen and snuck out through the dog door.

FLIP FLAP.

He had escaped the party and was on his way to becoming a real detective.

The back garden was eerily dark compared to the brightly lit house. Luckily, Arthur soon spotted the amber glow of Masha's eyes.

'All set for Operation Darryl?' she asked him.

Arthur shrugged. For a moment, he was torn between wanting to be a daring detective and wanting to return to the cheery warmth of the party.

'There are pigs in blankets, beef empanadas, and Chinese spring rolls indoors,' he mumbled.

'They'll still be some left when you get back,' Masha coaxed him. 'This is your moment! This is your first step to becoming a famous detective. So follow me!'

Masha had already planned the ground route they would take to Number 40. She knew that Arthur had no real climbing ability, but didn't want to offend the little fellow by telling him so.

'I'm not quite up to the high road tonight,' she lied. 'Some of those walls are treacherous. Remember Number 38 is very dark and that's where the vixen lives. It should be fine because she doesn't have any cubs. That's not to say she won't get territorial.'

'Don't worry, I can handle a vixen,' Arthur assured her.

'Great! Let's go, *Sherlock.*'

Just hearing the name of his sleuthing hero worked wonders. 'I'm right behind you, Detective Tawson,' said Arthur with renewed confidence.

The night mission was underway. Arthur couldn't help but admire Masha; she was remarkable at night. She was as clever as a Golden Retriever and as agile as a Border Collie. Effortlessly, she crawled between jagged, splintered fence panels, snaked through long grass, crept over mole hills and clawed through compost. Every now and then, she looked back at him to check that he was keeping up.

Occasionally, the little dog stumbled but he persevered and used his supersensitive sense of smell to navigate. All the different odours of damp soil, rain-soaked leaves and animal poo helped him draw a mental map of the whole area.

Without warning, the dark figure of a fox loomed in front of them. They had reached the back garden of Number 38. Immediately, Arthur began to growl and bare his canine teeth. He couldn't see the vixen very clearly but her large silhouette was frightening and her musky scent filled his snout.

Masha's tail was straight and spiky and her fur stood on end. She faced the vixen, hissing and spitting. She couldn't speak Fox but her body language was easily understood.

The garden was cloaked in darkness except for one distant light shining from a loft room high above their heads. Arthur growled louder, disturbed by a flash of fox fangs.

'Leave us alone vixen!' warned Arthur, speaking perfect Fox.

The vixen dropped the small mouse she'd been carrying in her mouth. 'This isn't your garden,' she retorted, lashing her tail. 'This is my garden, and you're the intruders! And don't even think about eating this mouse—I caught it so it's mine.'

Was this a foxy bluff or was this vixen serious about a fight? Arthur was much too full to eat a mouse but this didn't stop the fox from barking aggressively. Soon, the garden throbbed with growls and hisses, and the glint of sharp teeth and flashing eyes. Arthur and Masha stood side by side, making an impressive two-headed creature; they inflated their bodies to look bigger and edged towards the fox.

Unexpectedly, a bathroom light went on and streaked across the garden.

'Shut up out there!' came a gruff human voice from inside the house.

In all the confusion, the lucky mouse managed to escape and the vixen decided to make a hasty retreat. Arthur's body trembled and Masha frantically licked her fur, trying to regain her composure.

'That was awful and scary yet exhilarating,' Arthur whispered.

Moments later, the animal detectives made their way to the bottom of the garden and crawled under the fence to Number 40. They heard a rustle and, sure enough, when they looked up they spied two shadowy squirrels resting on the fence.

'Sausage and Mash at your service,' chorused Arthur and Masha.

'Hello fellas,' said Darryl. 'This is Meryl, my oldest soap and water.'

'Soap and water means daughter,' Arthur reminded Masha.

'Hello fellas,' Meryl chirped.

'We've bin 'ere a while, and seen nuffink,' commented Darryl.

'We're waiting for the feef,' said Meryl.

'He or she will turn up,' Arthur assured her. 'Then we'll have our culprit.'

Stealthily, Arthur and Masha hid themselves behind the musty compost heap. From this vantage point, they could spy on Darryl's not-so-secret hiding hole. Arthur peeked at the house at Number 40. It was bright and cheerful; lights glowed in the upstairs windows; and a twitch of his nose told him the people inside were eating chicken kebabs. He began wishing he, too, was warm and cosy, sharing a takeaway. The fine, soft fur on his tummy was cold and Masha's whiskers sparkled with icy water droplets.

'This isn't how I imagined a night watch,' Arthur grumbled. 'I thought it would be glamorous.'

'You'll never be a professional detective at this rate,' Masha chuckled.

PITTER-PATTER, PITTER-PATTER.

The pet detectives realised that they were about to meet Darryl's thief.

'I smell a hedgehog,' whispered Arthur. 'Should we pounce on it?'

'Let's wait and see what happens,' suggested Masha.

RUSTLE, CRUNCH, SNAP. The creature was getting closer.

'Do you speak Hedgehog?' Arthur asked Masha under his breath.

'Enough to get by,' she replied. 'Let's surround it or it'll get away. You wouldn't believe how fast a hedgehog can run!'

'I know! It's astounding,' recalled Arthur. 'Dylan showed me an animal video of a hedgehog dribbling a football!'

'You block its escape, I'll creep up behind it,' Masha instructed.

The hedgehog would never make a good spy; he was grunting and snuffling as noisily as a litter of piglets. Arthur wasn't too fond of hedgehogs. Last year, his cousin Bella, a wire-haired dachshund, suffered a horrible injury after playing with a hedgehog.

In the sky above them, wispy clouds drifted away and the full moon shone brightly into the garden. The pet detectives could now see what they were dealing with: they recognised the unmistakable shape of a very small hedgehog. The hedgehog was making such a commotion scratching and digging away at Darryl's winter food stash that he hadn't noticed he was completely surrounded.

'Freeze!' Arthur commanded.

'Don't move a spine!' Masha shouted.

Terrified, the hedgehog hissed and screamed. Masha knew instantly that this was a very young hedgehog, hardly old enough to be away from his mother. The hedgehog carried on screaming, which brought human faces to the windows at Number 40. Arthur, who thought his eardrums would explode, jumped back and yelped.

Masha took charge. 'Stop that!' she ordered, with a dangerous glint in her eyes. 'Stop that horrible sound!'

'Please let me go, don't eat me! I'm only a baby,' the hedgehog pleaded. 'I don't want any trouble.'

'Tell us your name, you little scamp!' Arthur growled at him.

'I'm Viggo,' replied the tiny creature.

'What are you doing here?' roared Masha.

'I'm taking a stroll,' whimpered Viggo. 'It's a lovely night.'

'Out for a stroll?' Masha quizzed him.

'But this isn't your food, is it?' stated Arthur. 'We think you're a thief!'

The hedgehog thrust out his prickles and tried to curl up into a spiky ball.

'Don't do that, young hog!' warned Masha. 'We need to talk to you.'

'Just talk to me?' asked Viggo fearfully. 'Not kill me? Not eat me?'

'I'm not like other cats—I'm almost a vegetarian,' explained Masha.

'Almost?' snivelled Viggo fretfully. Then he stared at the muscly dachshund and gasped.

'You needn't worry about me either,' said Arthur. 'First of all, I've just come from a party with delicious food. I ate my own dinner and then Granny's sausage roll. Second, my poor cousin Bella couldn't woof for a year after getting a hedgehog spine stuck in her snout! So you are ABSOLUTELY at the bottom of my menu too.'

Viggo uncurled his body and tucked in his spines. 'I'm only a juvenile hog, not much more than a baby. Mummy told me that cats are predators and dogs are nuisances.'

'Your mum is probably right—if rather rude,' said Masha.

'I'm surprised your well-informed mum didn't tell you that stealing is wrong!' Arthur snapped.

The hedgehog looked ashamed and turned away from the pet detectives.

Darryl and Meryl were perched comfortably on the fence, watching the whole scene. They were eating their acorns as though they had VIP seats at the cinema.

'This collection of nutritious food takes weeks to gather, and belongs to that big squirrel and his family,' Masha explained to Viggo. 'If you steal from this hidey-hole, you're robbing baby squirrels! They'll go hungry this winter.'

'That's right, Sausage 'n' Mash!' bellowed Meryl in a surprisingly loud voice.

'You've just earned yourself another acorn,' said Darryl, looking lovingly at his kit.

'Are you really Sausage and Mash, the pet detectives?' asked Viggo. 'Mummy says you have an excellent office at Number 22.'

'Thank you,' said Arthur modestly.

'Now I can I tell her you're the best-dressed pets I've ever met!' added Viggo.

Arthur beamed with pride. It was difficult to dislike such an observant hedgehog.

'Save your flattery,' Masha scolded him. 'You need to apologise to those two squirrels and promise not to steal from them or anyone else ever again!'

Viggo looked up at Darryl and Meryl and chirped, 'I'm sorry Big Squirrel and Little Squirrel and I won't do it again.'

Arthur wanted to be certain that Viggo had learned his lesson and, perhaps, show him some of his finest bow ties. 'I don't think it would be a bad idea if you had some lessons in animal etiquette,' he suggested.

Masha looked at Arthur in agreement.

'Et-tee-ket?' Viggo asked, puzzled.

'Yes, Viggo, we need to teach you the Animal Code,' said Arthur. 'All animals should live by it. It's about knowing the difference between right and wrong. Understanding why we need to share and care for our ecosystems, for our habitats, and for our planet.'

Masha was impressed by Arthur's speech. 'You know where our office is, young Viggo,' she said. 'We're open for business most weekdays.'

'Weekend times may vary,' Arthur added.

'Will I get treats to eat?' asked Viggo. 'We hedgehogs love cat and dog food. Not the gravy variety, the ones with jelly.'

'That could be arranged,' said Masha, 'but you'll have to earn it.'

Arthur was exhausted and famished when he finally got home. He was quite worn out from his nighttime mission. But before climbing the stairs, a quick inspection of his food bowl revealed a tasty chunk of cheese one of the partygoers had left him. When he got to his upstairs bed, with a full tummy, he fell asleep instantly and began dreaming.

In his dream, he was no longer Arthur the sophisticated pet detective; he was the hero of an action and adventure movie. At Number 38, he fended off a whole skulk of fearsome foxes single-handedly. At Number 40, he easily vanquished Viggo, no longer a harmless baby, but a vicious hedgehog monster with terrifying spines and vampire teeth. Returning home, Arthur was greeted by all his fans: Masha, Darryl, Cheryl, Meryl, Laurel, Zeus, Pinkie and Gemma. They were clapping and cheering, admiring his detective outfit, and offering him chicken.

Arthur had always had a lively imagination. What actually happened was less spectacular. Viggo had plodded back to his nest to tell his mum he'd misbehaved.

Darryl and Meryl, who'd been startled by a noise, had run away sending acorn shells flying like confetti. Masha had accompanied Arthur all the way to his dog door. Once she'd made sure he was safely indoors, she had made her own way home.

Chapter 6
Operation Viggo

Sausage and Mash headquarters sparkled in autumn sunshine after a sprinkling of rain. Inside, soft classical music played whilst Viggo completed his fourth and final training session in etiquette.

'What have you learned so far?' Arthur asked the junior hedgehog.

'Having etiquette is about good manners,' replied Viggo nervously.

'What else?' asked Masha, willing the tiny hedgehog to succeed.

'It's about sharing and caring,' Viggo remembered. 'Every creature is part of an animal community. If we all help one another, we can make our neighbourhood a better place.'

'Spot on,' Arthur grinned. He pointed to the Animal Code poster on the wall. 'Live by that code and things will work out swimmingly. You'll make your mum proud of you.'

Viggo mustered up all his energy and recited the pledge from memory.

'Not bad for an undomesticated hog,' Arthur whispered to Masha. He was unaccustomed to towering over any animal; standing beside Viggo made him feel important and almost kingly.

'Excellent work,' Masha told Viggo. 'You've remembered everything, and I am very impressed.'

'We don't want to hear that you've been stealing, lying or wandering about without your mum's permission,' Arthur warned.

Viggo's prickles quivered and quaked. The sausage dog was absolutely enormous!

Masha showed the little hog his reward for completing his homework: a dish filled with dog food *in jelly*. Instantly, Viggo's mood brightened and he greedily snorted his way through the succulent morsels. In no time, the dish was almost empty and he was fast asleep on a woolly bobble hat.

Like proud parents, Arthur and Masha smiled at the small creature.

'I consider this a huge success,' beamed Arthur. 'It's a great achievement for us both.'

'Absolutely! If Viggo remembers his Animal Code he'll grow up into a wonderful adult hog one day,' agreed Masha.

The classical music faded at the exact same moment that Viggo let out a colossal hiccup followed by two noisy snorts. The pet detectives glanced at one another in surprise.

Masha broke the awkward silence. 'Do you remember I told you about my brother?' she asked.

Arthur delved into his memory bank. Despite his best efforts, he was distracted; his nose was being tickled by the delectable jelly in Viggo's dish.

Masha gazed at him with her piercing amber eyes.

'Of course, I know you have a brother,' insisted Arthur. 'He's called Timmy, and he lives at Number 9.'

'Timmy!' gasped Masha in disbelief.

'No, sorry, he's Tommy!' said Arthur with full confidence.

'My brother's called *Tumbler*,' said Masha impatiently. 'He lives *nine houses* away from me at Number 50. Don't you remember, I told you that Tumbler's back garden looks out onto the park?'

'Oh that's right,' Arthur mumbled, still distracted. 'Don't you two get together every Thursday?'

'Every *Tuesday*,' sighed Masha.

Arthur threw her a bemused look. 'Has something happened to your brother?' he wondered.

'No, he's fine,' she said. 'I told him all about the stakeout at Number 40.'

Arthur nodded and smiled.

'Tumbler has offered to help us whenever he can,' explained Masha.

'How kind! Thank him from me,' said Arthur. His left ear began to twitch as it tuned in to Daisy's high-pitched singing—more like wailing—coming from the house. 'In fact, tell Tumbler that for every new client he sends us he can have his choice of treats.'

Masha's eyes twinkled with mischief. 'Yesterday, Tumbler was in the back garden watching life go by in the park...'

'How pleasant for him,' commented Arthur. 'I've always wished we had a view of the park.'

Masha proceeded to list everything that Tumbler had seen from his back garden:

cheeky squirrels; a couple of seagulls; children racing their scooters; people playing football; someone's kite getting tangled in a tree; and a worried lady searching for her naughty, runaway dog.

'Yes, things like that tend to happen in our local park,' muttered Arthur.

'Then there was a little girl, who cycled past on a bicycle that was much too big for her,' continued Masha with a giggle. 'Then there was a lively game of tag.'

Arthur began to wonder if Masha wanted to win first prize for The… Slowest… Story… Ever… Told… By… A… Cat.

'That's when Tumbler saw you in the park,' said Masha.

'I wasn't in the park yesterday!' protested Arthur.

'That's right! What I mean is, Tumbler saw the dog who wasn't you.'

'Tumbler saw me but it wasn't me?' asked Arthur, feeling as cloudy as the weather.

After a perfect pause, Masha went on: 'Tumbler ran up to the sausage dog he thought was you and said, "How's the Sausage and Mash business? I heard all about your night ambush and I'm really impressed." But this little dog didn't have a clue what he was talking about.'

'He didn't...? Why should he? Who was he?' inquired Arthur, suddenly distracted by the delicious aroma of chicken casserole coming from the kitchen.

Still, Masha wouldn't be rushed. Like any good storyteller, she wanted to build suspense. She licked her elegant paws then glanced at Viggo, who, still snuffling like a baby, had buried himself deeper into the bobble hat.

'Is that the whole story?' snapped Arthur. 'If it isn't, I'd like to go and rummage for snacks in the kitchen before you start Part Two. I'm afraid I've got a bit peckish.'

After a deep yoga stretch, Masha carried on: 'Although you and Tumbler haven't met, he knows exactly what you look like. I've told him everything about you. So when Tumbler saw this other dog he mistook him for you because he looked just like the *you* I've described!'

'Obviously, I'm not the only red-haired dachshund in our suburb,' said Arthur. 'Although, I'm probably the best-dressed.'

Masha playfully flashed her amber eyes at him before continuing: 'This dachshund clone of yours said to Tumbler, "Did you say sausage and mash? I want some sausage and mash. I'm starving! Actually, I could eat ten jumbo sausages and a pile of mash taller than an Egyptian pyramid!'

Arthur's chestnut brown eyes widened with alarm. 'It was Jim, wasn't it?' he gasped.

Masha nodded gently.

'It was that rascally hound with illegally bad manners!' wailed Arthur.

'It gets worse,' promised Masha.

Arthur's tail plummeted like a wet firework. 'Oh no...'

'The real reason Tumbler thought that Jim was you, the famous neighbourhood detective, was because of his clothes.'

'What was Jim wearing?' yelped Arthur.

'A deerstalker hat and a tweedy cape,' said Masha.

'*My* deerstalker hat and *my* tweedy cape,' repeated Arthur grumpily. 'So that snivelling scoundrel and his lush friend really did steal my outfit!! That miserable excuse for a dachshund has no business wearing haute couture! He's the dog world's worst listener! I'd like to lock that wrinkly-chinned rascal in a kennel for a year with nothing to eat but Della's vegetarian biscuits!'

Masha was stunned. 'Arthur, you'll wake Viggo and half the neighbourhood if you don't calm down. Take a breath.'

Arthur took a few slow, deep breaths to regain the composure expected of a pedigree dachshund. 'Give me a minute,' he said to Masha, and left the office.

Through the glass doors, Masha watched Arthur power walk across the grass to the far end of the garden. There, he barked angrily (Masha couldn't hear what he said).

On his return, he weaved around Daisy's overturned scooter, Dylan's deflated football, and Della's muddy wellies and waited for Masha to join him outside headquarters.

'I'm glad that Jim's been taking such good care of my outfit,' said Arthur coolly. 'But I'll need it back now. We'll show Jim and Lewis how *real* detectives get results. It takes more than just "looking the business" to be a super sleuth.'

'Whatever it takes, I'm right beside you,' Masha guaranteed him.

Viggo woke up after an outrageously loud snort. Still feeling drowsy, he stumbled through the dog flap to join Arthur and Masha in the garden. The little hedgehog hadn't realised that the woolly bobble hat had fastened itself to his spines and was dragging behind him. He looked up at the pet detectives with a crooked grin.

'Did I miss anything?' he asked them.

Chapter 7
Operation Reclaim Outfit

The Sausage and Mash duo knew that Jim might seem like a silly dog with bad manners but he was very cunning; Lewis was fun and lively but, like all corgis, was much stronger than his size suggested. For Operation Reclaim Outfit to work, nothing could be left to chance and timings had to be exact. After all, Arthur didn't have the same freedom as Masha to come and go.

OPERATION RECLAIM OUTFIT

<u>Detectives:</u> Sausage and Mash
<u>Assistant:</u> Tumbler

<u>Ruse:</u> Tumbler invites Jim and Lewis to his back garden for a picnic (cheddar cheese, Gloucester cheese, sliced ham, meatballs).

The Plan

4.30 p.m. The picnic starts.
4.35 p.m. Masha arrives, and asks Jim to be the new sausage in Sausage and Mash Agency.
4.40 p.m. Dylan is busy. Arthur squeezes through the railings to interrupt the picnic.

<u>Outcomes:</u>
Arthur gets his outfit back.
Jim and Lewis disappear FOREVER!
(Tumbler saves some picnic food for Arthur!)

Today was the ideal day for the mission because it was Dylan's turn to take Arthur to the park. Whenever Dylan went to the park, he spent at least twenty minutes talking to his girlfriend Anjali on his mobile phone. That would give Arthur plenty of time to sneak away to Tumbler's back garden, surprise cowardly Jim, and seize his detective outfit.

Today, Arthur was happy about everything. He had a hearty breakfast, followed by a generous brunch, followed by a chat with the tropical fish in the aquarium.

'It's an important day,' Arthur told them. 'Of course, every day is important but today is going to be magnificent. I've concocted a brilliant plan to reclaim what's rightfully mine.'

At midday, Arthur met Masha under the oak tree at the bottom of the garden. They wanted to run through the final details of their daring offensive. The blustery weather sent autumn leaves swirling around them like whirling dervishes.

'At 4:30 p.m., Jim and Lewis will follow Tumbler into the back garden via the side alley,' Arthur said secretively.

'Check,' Masha replied in a whisper. 'I'll arrive at 4:35 p.m. and tell Jim that he looks amazing in his detective outfit. Then I'll casually ask if he'd be willing to replace you.'

Wrinkling his nose in disgust, Arthur continued with the plan: 'At 4:40 p.m., Dylan will make his phone call. That's when I'll make a dash for Tumbler's garden. I'll squeeze through the gap in between the bent railings. It'll be a big, bold entrance! I can't wait to see the expression on Jim's face!'

'That's true,' agreed Masha. 'It'll be a real shock for Jim and Lewis to see you. You'll confront them and demand the return of your detective outfit. Tumbler will tell the villains to clear off, and you'll return to Dylan who'll be none the wiser. I'll keep your outfit safe and bring it back here first thing tomorrow morning.'

'It's a great plan,' Arthur said eagerly. 'And Tumbler won't forget to save me some ham and cheddar, will he?'

'Of course not,' Masha assured him.

'I can't wait to see myself in my deerstalker hat and tweed cape,' sighed Arthur.

'We're Sausage and Mash!' exclaimed Masha. 'We're the pawsome pet detectives who smash crime.'

'And we're about to *smash this case*!' declared Arthur.

The hallway clock told Arthur it was 4:15 p.m. The dachshund was wearing his serious, navy blue bow tie. Grabbing his lead between his teeth, he scurried upstairs, and nudged Dylan's bedroom door open with his snout.

Normally at this point, Dylan would tickle his pet under the chin, throw on his trainers, and race him to the front door. Dylan did none of these things. He was lying on his bed, arguing with Anjali on his phone!

'GET UP DYLAN!' barked Arthur. 'YOU HAVE TO GET UP AND TAKE ME TO THE PARK!'

Dylan was unsympathetic. 'No walk for us today, Arty-Smarty,' he murmured. 'I've got man troubles.'

The rhythmic tick-tock of the hallway clock began to boom in Arthur's ears like claps of thunder. It was 4:17 p.m. and it would take ten minutes to get to the park— he had to move fast. He snatched up his lead and darted into Daisy's room. She wasn't there! Arthur remembered she was at her best friend's birthday party.

It was 4:18 p.m. Arthur rushed down the stairs and almost took a tumble on the last step. Mum and Dad wouldn't be home for another hour. His last hope—his *only* hope—was Della. She would be home any minute now...

Sure enough the key turned in the front door. Della came in listening to music. She was carrying her trainers in one hand and her shiny backpack in the other. She looked exhausted after double PE and an after-school netball match. THINGS WEREN'T LOOKING GOOD FOR ARTHUR! Convincing Della that she needed more exercise was going to be VERY tricky. Drawing on his acting skills, Arthur whimpered and tilted his head, wearing a well-practised, forlorn expression.

'Oh no! What's wrong, Arthur?' Della asked. She dropped her belongings onto the floor. 'Are you hurt?' Puzzled, she inspected the dachshund's ears and all four paws. 'You don't look hurt… Didn't Dylan take you out?'

Arthur raised his eyebrows, dipped his chin, made his tail droop, and snivelled.

'I would take you out, Arty,' said Della quietly, 'but I'm so tired!'

Arthur yelped, whined and whistled.

'Poor Arty-Smarty, you really want to go out!' noticed Della.

Arthur practically nodded.

'Okay, I'll take you to the park,' she said. 'Let me drink some water then I'll change back into my trainers.'

It was 4:26 p.m. Arthur had no time to waste. As soon as they were outside, he propelled Della to the park like a horse pulling a chariot.

'This must be an emergency,' Della said, trying to keep up with him. 'I'm going to have words with Dylan. We all have to be responsible pet owners.'

Unfortunately, one of Della's trainers worked itself loose so she came to a sudden halt—and so did Arthur. She needed to stop, find a wall, sit down and put her trainer back on with a secure double bow.

It was 4:38 p.m. and they were on the move again. Arthur yanked Della through the iron gates at the park entrance. He was grateful to his sister for walking him but he had ABSOLUTELY NO TIME to listen to her reel off facts about every different tree they passed.

'See that willow over there?' she said enthusiastically. 'Do you know that its roots can spread out as far as three times its length?'

Arthur heard someone in the park say it was 4:39 p.m. In horror, he realised that he had one measly minute to escape from Della and get to Tumbler's garden. He tugged at his lead and felt his collar loosening but this only annoyed Della.

'If you don't behave, we're going straight back home!' she warned him.

Their tug of war continued. Della pulled one way and Arthur pulled the other. Della pulled harder so Arthur pulled even harder. He was determined to press on with the business of smashing crime.

'That's it!' shouted Della decisively. 'We're going home as a consequence.'

All of a sudden, Arthur spotted five familiar squirrels: Darryl and Cheryl, and their kits Meryl, Laurel and Zeus. The squirrels, who'd been lounging in the oak tree at the bottom of Arthur's garden, had overheard every detail of Operation Reclaim Outfit. They'd even followed Arthur and Della all the way to the park. Now, they felt it was their duty to surround Della so that Arthur could make his escape.

'I don't have anything to feed you squirrels,' apologised Della. 'Anyway, I don't agree with people giving you unhealthy snacks. You're wild animals that need to stay wild. Feeding you could turn you into pests and make you dependent on humans! That's only going to put you in danger.'

The squirrels didn't give up. Darryl and Cheryl hopped around Della's feet while Meryl, Laurel and Zeus grabbed at her laces.

In all the commotion, Della hadn't noticed that she'd dropped Arthur's dog lead.

'Run for it, mate!' Darryl shouted to Arthur. 'We'll keep Della busy!'

'I'll be eternally grateful, Darryl!' yelled the dachshund.

Arthur galloped across the grass, his lead swinging behind him like a lasso and his ears flapping like kites in a storm. Della's cries of 'Arthur! Come back here!' gradually faded into the distance.

Finally, Arthur, panting and heart racing, found himself on the park side of Tumbler's back garden. After a frantic search, he identified the bent railings and slithered through the gap.

Preparing to make a dramatic entrance—and take Jim and Lewis by complete surprise—Arthur's lead got caught on some unruly brambles. He pulled himself free before stumbling into the garden looking dusty and dishevelled.

Lewis, who was chomping on his second pack of ham, casually looked up at Arthur. 'You've missed out, boyo,' he said with his mouth full. 'All the best stuff's gone!'

Then Arthur caught a glimpse of Jim, in his detective suit, twirling like a fashion model. He seemed to be enjoying Masha and Tumbler's attention.

'Look, I won't promise you anything,' Jim told Masha. 'I might be the new sausage in Sausage and Splash. But I might also not be. Just let me finish my picnic.'

'Look, Jimmy boy, it's your twin,' chortled Lewis, glancing in Arthur's direction then crunching into a chicken bone.

The two, almost identical, dachshunds walked towards each other. They stood snout to snout. It was obvious by now that it had got serious: there was going to be a Staring Contest! Not an ordinary staring contest, but an EPIC STARING SHOWDOWN, which is always a big deal in the dog world. Who would look away first? Who could hold their nerve the longest? The other animals gathered around to see who'd win.

'Arty-Smarty? Where are you, Arty-Smarty?' called Della, from somewhere in the park.

Embarrassed, Arthur fixed his gaze on his opponent. He hoped that no one noticed that his ears twitched every time he heard his nickname being called.

Tumbler was mesmerised by the two dachshunds. 'They're mirror images of each other,' he muttered to Masha.

'They are quite alike,' she agreed quietly. 'But keep that to yourself.'

Unbelievably, Jim looked more like Arthur than the *real* Arthur. The *real* Arthur was bedraggled; his bow tie was crooked, his face was smeared, and his lead was twisted

around his hind legs. Despite this, Arthur stood tall and didn't flinch. He carried on staring straight into Jim's eyes.

'You think you're the bee's cheese,' Jim pouted at Arthur. 'And too cool for pool!'

'The bee's *knees*?' suggested Masha.

'Too cool for *school*, perhaps?' added Tumbler.

'Whatever!' snorted Jim. 'Look at the detective now.'

'He's like something the cat dragged in!' said Lewis, swallowing several meatballs.

Irritated but controlling his anger, Arthur was determined to be the winner of the staring contest. He just had to win for decent, law-abiding dachshunds everywhere.

Then, without any warning, Jim dashed off to retrieve a secret packet of cheese that he'd hidden from the other picnickers. His departure signalled the end of the staring contest. Arthur took a moment to relish his victory and Tumbler congratulated him.

'Where did you get your outfit?' Masha casually asked Jim.

'We found it,' replied Lewis on Jim's behalf.

Jim nodded, his mouth full of cheese slices. 'It fits me better than Lewis,' he spluttered, 'so I kept it. Finders keepers, losers jeepers.'

'Losers *weepers*!' Masha chimed in.

'Well, wherever we found it, you've gotta admit Jim looks awesome and amazing,' boasted Lewis.

'I look lush!' jeered Jim. 'I look just like Shamrock Gnomes!' He wiggled for attention.

Watching this silly spectacle, Arthur suddenly had a bright idea.

'I used to want a detective outfit,' he admitted, winking at Masha and Tumbler. 'That was before I ordered a float coat life jacket. It's reflective and it's got several strong pockets. It's made for all kinds of weather conditions. I can't wait to wear it on my next expedition.'

'Oh yes,' Masha agreed with a mischievous grin. 'I saw a picture of Arthur's flotation coat on the internet. It's *very* expensive because it's waterproof yet breathable.'

'Oh I know the one,' Tumbler piped up, happy to be in on the ruse. 'I've heard that all the celebrity dogs have one. It's got style, it's got bling!'

'A sausage dog could easily be mistaken for a spy or a secret agent like James Bond in a jacket like that,' said Arthur.

Jim's eyes widened. 'Ooh, I could be like Flames Pond,' he gasped. 'Or be a secretly aging gent on a lifeboat.' He beckoned for

Lewis to come over so that he could whisper in his ear.

'So you've ordered another package?' Lewis asked Arthur, trying to sound flippant.

'Yes, I have,' lied Arthur. 'In fact, I'd like to stay but I really should get home. My new jacket's probably being delivered as we speak! I can't wait to try it on!

'I don't want to wear this detective suit anymore,' whined Jim. 'It's all itchy and it's got no shiny bits! I want something with blong and string packets.'

In no time, Jim was undressing and chucking his deerstalker hat and tweed cape onto the ground.

'Looks like Jim doesn't want that woolly outfit, boyo,' Lewis said to Arthur. 'If it's not right for Jimmy, why don't you have it? It'd probably look better on an older, stouter sausage dog like you.'

'How very kind of you,' said Arthur, rolling his eyes. 'It's not every day that a corgi gives me a birthday present when it isn't even my birthday!'

'Cooee!' Jim interrupted sharply.

'So we're off,' announced Lewis. 'Thanks for the grub but we just remembered we have another party to get to.'

'Don't let us keep you,' said Masha.

Jim followed Lewis down the side alley.

Arthur, Masha and Tumbler shared a jubilant moment of relief.

'Sausage and Mash the Pawsome Pet Detectives Smash Crime!' chirped Arthur.

'With the help of my wonderful brother,' purred Masha.

'I was happy to help—it was a lot of fun,' replied Tumbler with a giggle.

'Huge thanks!' smiled Arthur. 'You've done me a great service! Let's all get together soon at Sausage and Mash headquarters for refreshments and treats. We have meat and vegetarian options.'

Tumbler nodded his appreciation, then added: 'Do you think Jim and Lewis learned anything useful today?'

'I'm not sure,' confessed Arthur. 'But Operation Bad-Mannered Dachshund will have to wait.'

'I agree,' said Masha. 'Anyway, just imagine their faces...'

'When they realise there's nothing on my doorstep for them to steal!' hooted Arthur. 'Finally...' His eyes lingered on the pile of sophisticated clothes on the ground. 'The pet detective is reunited with his brand new outfit! After it's been thoroughly washed and dried, I'll put it on. I'll look dignified and—'

'So there you are!' a thunderous voice boomed across the garden.

Everyone saw Arthur's furious but relieved sister Della on the other side of the railings.

'I think the picnic's over,' whispered Masha.

'Yes, it's definitely hometime,' agreed Arthur. 'Until tomorrow.'

'Until tomorrow,' repeated Masha. 'When I'll bring your suit over.'

Waddling towards the railings, his lead still dragging behind him, Arthur seized on another brilliant idea. He snatched one of the empty meat packets between his teeth.

Della's cheeks flushed with anger. 'You ran away from me for a packet of processed meat!' she gasped. 'Oh Arthur, I'm so disappointed in you! I really hope you weren't bothering those poor cats. I'm telling everyone you need some serious dog training. But before any of that, we're going to recycle that plastic packaging!'

Arthur was marched over to the recycling bin. He was sorry for upsetting Della. She was a vegetarian but he liked her a great deal. Even though she fed him sawdust biscuits, and nagged at him, it was only because she wanted to protect the environment. So, in her own way, Della was a bit of a hero, and a bit like Sherlock Holmes.

When they got home, Arthur entertained Della with his best trick. He played fetch with his chewy banana toy to make her laugh. Afterwards, she seemed to have forgotten all about the running away incident and didn't mention any extra dog training.

Operation Reclaim Outfit had been a success. Now it was Masha's turn to smarten up her look. She always wore a plain collar—she should wear a bow tie. Arthur had seen one that would complement her amber eyes. After all, if Sausage and Mash were going to keep on smashing crime they would *both* need to look like professionals. What had Darryl called it? Oh yes, they both needed to 'look the business' from now on.

SAUSAGE AND MASH PET DETECTIVES SERIES

Sausage and Mash Pawsome Pet Detectives

Sausage and Mash at Halloween

Sausage and Mash at Christmas

Sausage and Mash at Easter

Sausage and Mash on the Beach

Visit Sausage and Mash's website at
www.sausageandmashpetdetectives.com
for activities and downloads!

ABOUT THE AUTHOR

Eva Bea Knight is a part-time teacher and writer/illustrator, who lives in London. When she isn't walking her sausage dog or cat-sitting, she loves reading detective novels, watching mystery films, and planning her next book.

Celebrate Halloween with the Pawsome Pet Detectives!

Find out who's stolen Honey the Persian cat's precious collar. Discover why Chilli the Chihuahua is being haunted by a ghost with furry feet.

Don't miss out on the spooky fun in the next book in the series.

Sausage and Mash at Halloween

Printed in Great Britain
by Amazon